THE DINOSAUR THAT POOPED THE BED!

For Buzz, who poops more than Dino —T. F.
I would like to dedicate this book to the twinkle in my eye. —D. P.
For Codie & Kyle —G. P.

ALADDIN

An imprint of Simon & Schuster Children's Publishing Division

1230 Avenue of the Americas, New York, New York 10020

This Aladdin hardcover edition November 2018

Copyright © 2015 by Tom Fletcher and Dougie Poynter

Illustrations by Garry Parsons

Originally published in Great Britain by Red Fox.

Published by arrangement with Penguin Random House Children's UK

All rights reserved, including the right of reproduction in whole or in part in any form.

ALADDIN and related logo are registered trademarks of Simon & Schuster, Inc.

For information about special discounts for bulk purchases, please contact
Simon & Schuster Special Sales at 1-866-506-1949 or business@simonandschuster.com.

The Simon & Schuster Speakers Bureau can bring authors to your live event. For more information or to book an event
contact the Simon & Schuster Speakers Bureau at 1-866-248-3049 or visit our website at www.simonspeakers.com.

Manufactured in China 0818 SCP

10 9 8 7 6 5 4 3 2 1

Library of Congress Control Number 2018933956

ISBN 978-1-4814-9870-8 (hc)

ISBN 978-1-4814-9871-5 (eBook)

THE DINOSAUR THAT POOPED THE BED!

Tom Fletcher & Dougie Poynter
Illustrated by Garry Parsons

ALADDIN

NEW YORK LONDON TORONTO SYDNEY NEW DELHI

It was one of those slow, boring, dull afternoons,
When Danny said, "I know—let's watch some cartoons!"
But then Danny's mom cast a shadow of gloom.
"You can't watch TV till you've cleaned up your room."

They slumped up the stairs; they were so very grumpy,
  And stood in their room at the foot of Mount Dumpy.
"Cleaning this mess will take thousands of years,"
  Said Danny while desperately holding back tears.

Unless they were going to clean up forever,
They needed a plan—a plan that was clever.

And then an idea popped into Danny's head.
"Why clean up this mess? You can eat it instead!"

So Dinosaur opened its mouth like a bin:
Dan scooped up the mess and he threw it all in.

Toys from the top and lots underneath
Were chucked in and chomped by the dinosaur's teeth.

It chewed Danny's shoes, it could not get enough
Of teddies and cuddly stuff made of fluff.
The dinosaur sucked every toy Danny threw,
But the more the mess shrank, the more Dinosaur grew.

Shirts, pants, and socks, little soldiers of tin . . .
  Dan laughed as he watched Dino shovel it in.
His fluffy pet hamster, along with its cage,
  Was swallowed in Dinosaur's mess-munching rage.

It smushed the CDs, which, on reflection,
   Were far from the greatest of record collections.
So Dan didn't mind—it all had to go
   If they wanted to kick back and watch TV shows. . . .

To Dino the bed looked just like a burger,
    As diamonds would look to the greediest burglar.
In one dino-bite the bed disappeared—
    No mess left in sight, the whole room had been cleared.

Danny's room was as clean as a bedroom could be.
"At last we can finally watch some TV!"
But Dinosaur's tummy cast a shadow of doom:
It was full to the brim with the mess of Dan's room!

Dino was wedged in between floor and ceiling.
It couldn't believe how full it was feeling.

It started to worry; it started to panic:
Never before had it been more gigantic!

The dinosaur's bottom was bigger than Norway,
So big and so fat it was blocking the doorway!

Then Dan started crying.

His nose dripped with snot.

They were stuck in their room
and the TV was not!

With pillows and quilts in the dinosaur's gut,
Its brain didn't have full control of its butt!

It knew that there wasn't a thing it could do.

One way or another,
it needed to . . .

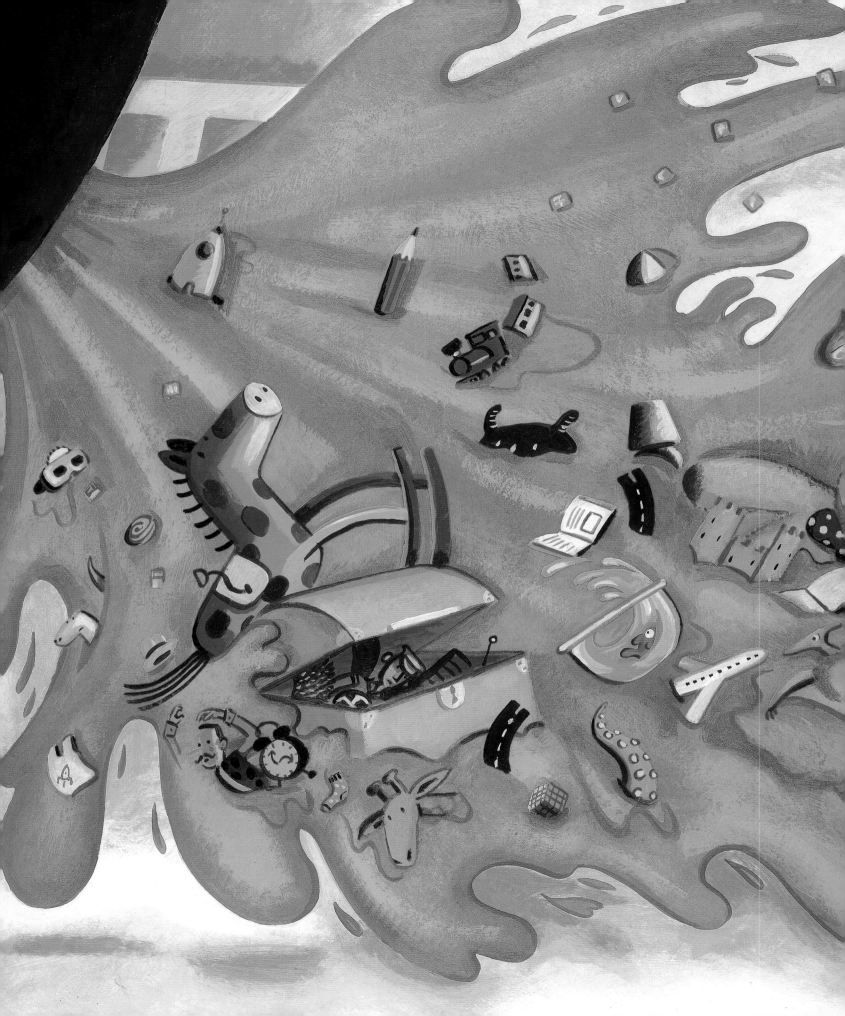

The dinosaur pooped more than ever before—
    All the mess they had cleared was now back on the floor.
Shoes, pants, and teddies, and soldiers and socks,
    With smelly poo lumps filling Danny's toy box.

Then Danny saw Dinosaur's face turning red
And knew the next thing to be pooped was his bed.
It sprang from its butt with a bounce and a bump
Right back to its place at the base of Mount Dump.

Now that Dino was empty, he unblocked the door,
Where Mommy was standing, more mad than before.
They looked at the mess all around where they stood
And knew they'd been naughty—and naughty's not good.

So they picked up their mops and mopped up the disaster.
Two cleaning together is always much faster.

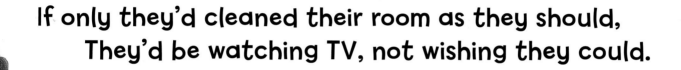

If only they'd cleaned their room as they should,
They'd be watching TV, not wishing they could.

So remember, the next time you're glued to the screen,
You can't watch cartoons if your bedroom's not clean!